OC

MG 4.0 lpt.

The Spy Who Came North from the Pole

The Spy Who Came North from the Pole:

MR. PIN, Vol. III

by Mary Elise Monsell
illustrated by Eileen Christelow

For Matteson
Library
Mary Elise Monsell

Atheneum   1993   New York

Maxwell Macmillan Canada
Toronto
Maxwell Macmillan International
New York   Oxford   Singapore   Sydney

*With high regards to David and Derek,
who know how to keep their
fingers on the seams*
—Mr. Pin

Text copyright © 1993 by Mary Elise Monsell
Illustrations copyright © 1993 by Eileen Christelow

Atheneum
Macmillan Publishing Company
866 Third Avenue
New York, NY 10022

Maxwell Macmillan Canada, Inc.
1200 Eglinton Avenue East
Suite 200
Don Mills, Ontario M3C 3N1

Macmillan Publishing Company is part of the Maxwell
Communication Group of Companies.

First edition
Printed in the United States of America
10 9 8 7 6 5 4 3 2 1

Library of Congress Cataloging-in-Publication Data
Monsell, Mary Elise.
The spy who came north from the Pole : Mr. Pin vol. III / by Mary
Elise Monsell; illustrated by Eileen Christelow.—1st ed.
p.   cm.
Summary: Mr. Pin, the rock hopper penguin detective in Chicago,
investigates two cases involving gargoyles and baseball.
ISBN 0-689-31754-9
[1. Penguins—Fiction. 2. Chicago (Ill.)—Fiction. 3. Mystery
and detective stories.] I. Christelow, Eileen, ill. II. Title.
PZ7.M7626Sp   1993
[Fic]—dc20   92-24646

Contents

The Spy Who Came North from the Pole

1

The sky was dark. The air was cold and foggy. It had been days since a rock hopper penguin had left the South Pole and made his way north to Chicago.

A black wing pulled the bus cord at Wabash Street. The driver watched as the penguin stepped into the fog. Strange. He thought that penguin looked familiar.

"Mind your step," the driver said. The penguin snarled back.

The door creaked shut and the bus headed west. The rock hopper headed north.

He was mostly black and white, with long yellow plumes on both sides of his head. He carried a mysterious brown bag under his wing.

Suddenly an elevated train screeched to a stop. A tall man in a trench coat came up to the railing and tossed a small box over the side. As the train screeched away, the rock hopper picked up the box. There was chocolate inside.

"*Frango mints!*" he said out loud. He took a magnifying glass out of his brown bag and looked more closely. There was a note inside the box. The rock hopper quickly ate the chocolates, then read the note:

CODEBOOK   CLUE   IN GARGOYLE

He got the idea all right. The clue he was looking for was hidden in a gargoyle. Now he just needed to find the right one. But where? Those strange carved-stone creatures were on buildings all over the city. Not only that, but they were usually up very high. And penguins don't fly.

It was also a little strange that the clue to the whereabouts of the codebook was in a gargoyle to begin with. But in any case, his plan seemed to be working.

"Looks like I arrived in Chicago just in time," he said out loud.

Just ahead was a diner—Smiling Sally's Good Food. The penguin outside saw another penguin sitting in a booth near the window. I wonder, thought the rock hopper, what would have happened if *that* penguin had seen this box first?

"Too late," he said out loud again. "But on the other hand, maybe he *should* see it . . . or one almost like it."

4

With sinister plans forming in his mind, the rock hopper penguin chuckled softly to himself, turned away from the diner, and disappeared into the fog. A moment later the lights in Smiling Sally's Diner went out.

2

It was foggy again the next day. The thick, wet air rolled down the sidewalks like sleepwalking ghosts. It would have been a day to be inside Smiling Sally's warm and friendly diner. But Mr. Pin and Maggie were somewhere else.

The two detectives were on the second floor of an old warehouse. They were looking for new stools for Smiling Sally's Diner. The warehouse belonged to Maggie's uncle Otis, who lived on the top floor. He sold an odd assortment of things that he rescued from buildings about to be torn down.

Maggie and Mr. Pin stood between a row of iron fences and old bathtubs with feet. Next to the fences and bathtubs were rows and rows of pillars, carved doors, marble fireplaces, stained-glass windows, restaurant booths, stools, sinks, doorknobs, hinges, and even staircases. Inside each bathtub was a gargoyle.

"This place is spooky," said Maggie as she looked at the peculiar expressions on the gargoyles' faces. "It's weird seeing old bathtubs all lined up and no one around to take a bath. And what are these things? They look like monsters."

"They're gargoyles," said Mr. Pin. "Some gargoyles look like monsters. Some just look like animals. You've seen them decorating old buildings, sometimes at the very top."

"I don't know how Otis can live here," said Maggie.

The knotted floorboards creaked.

Maggie shivered. "We should get the diner stools for Sally and go home. This place is giving me nightmares, and I'm not even asleep yet."

A low, groaning rumble shook the building. An elevator shuddered as it was lowered slowly down the shaft at the end of the row of bathtubs. A grated door opened, and a short, balding man wearing a striped vest stepped out.

"Uncle Otis!" shouted Maggie. "I'm glad to see you. Any minute now I was sure I was going to see a ghost."

"Hasn't been one here for a few months," said

Uncle Otis. Only half of his mouth turned up in a smile.

"This is Mr. Pin," said Maggie.

"Detective Pin. Reasonable rates," said the rock hopper penguin, tipping his checked cap.

Crash!!

"What was that?" asked Otis.

"A ghost!" cried Maggie.

"No," said Mr. Pin, darting between columns. "Someone dropped a gargoyle."

"A thief?" asked Otis.

"I don't know," said Mr. Pin.

"I thought I heard breathing before, and it wasn't ours," said Maggie.

Maggie and Otis rushed over to where Mr. Pin was examining an odd-shaped stone face that had been broken into several pieces.

"What is it?" asked Maggie.

"It used to be a gargoyle," said Mr. Pin.

"So where's the thief now?" asked Otis.

"A thief is only one possibility," corrected Mr. Pin.

But just then they heard running footsteps. A dark figure stepped into the elevator.

"Over there!" said Mr. Pin, pointing with his wing. They ran to the elevator, but it was too late. The door had squeaked shut.

"We'll take the stairs," directed Mr. Pin. The two detectives raced down the steep stairs, followed more slowly by Uncle Otis. They made it to the first floor just in time to see someone very short step through the fog and onto a waiting bus. Maggie and Mr. Pin watched as the driver, who was wearing a trench coat, pulled the bus away from the curb.

He was getting away!

Mr. Pin held up his wing to signal for a cab speeding around the corner. The cab screeched to a stop. Mr. Pin and Maggie climbed in.

"Follow that bus," said Mr. Pin to the driver.

"Sure, mister. No problem."

"I've never seen a bus driver wearing a trench coat," said Maggie.

"Interesting," said Mr. Pin. "Not only that, but I think the driver was actually waiting for whoever it was who smashed the gargoyle."

The bus zigzagged north, then east toward the lake.

"Strange bus route," said the driver.

"Strange," said Maggie. "I think that bus has only one passenger."

"*That* is a strange bus," said Mr. Pin. "But we'd better hurry. It's headed toward the bridge."

10

"Sure," said the cabdriver.

The taxi stayed close, but the bus was fast and the fog was thick.

"The drawbridge is going up!" shouted Maggie as they reached the Chicago River.

"I might just make it," said the driver.

"Not necessary," said Mr. Pin. And the taxi squealed to a stop just short of the rising bridge. The bus had made it over just in time.

"Whew! Thank goodness we stopped," said Maggie.

"Say, mister . . . ," said the driver.

"Mr. Pin," corrected the rock hopper.

"And I'm Maggie."

"I'm Gus," said the driver. "Glad to meet you. Say, when the bridge comes down, do you want me to keep going, or can I take you somewhere else?"

"Somewhere else, please. We've lost the bus," said Mr. Pin. "Smiling Sally's Diner on Monroe."

"I know the place. Food's good, and you meet interesting people," said Gus.

"I live there," said Mr. Pin.

"You do? Say, you must be the famous rock hopper penguin detective Mister. . . uh . . . Pen."

11

"Pin."

"Is Pen short for pencil?"

"No," said Mr. Pin. "Pin is just short, Gus."

"Like penguins, Mr. Pen?"

"Pin."

"Right. Well," Gus went on, "I guess this ride is on me. No charge. Just like Smiling Sally always says, no reason why big cities can't have big hearts. Right, Pen?"

"Right. And thanks, Ges."

3

Back at the diner, Maggie, Mr. Pin, and the taxi driver named Gus were all trying to explain to Smiling Sally what had happened when the two detectives had gone to buy diner stools from Uncle Otis.

"First it was spooky," said Maggie. "Then it got really spooky. Then Uncle Otis showed up."

"Did he help you find some nice stools for the diner, dear?" asked Smiling Sally, passing around fresh cinnamon rolls.

"He didn't have a chance," said Maggie. "You see, that was when we found the gargoyle."

"I don't think I really want a gargoyle," said Sally.

"Anyway, it was broken," said Maggie.

"Oh dear," said Sally. "Was it valuable?"

"Could be," said Mr. Pin. "We don't know yet. But that was when we heard footsteps."

"Footsteps?"

"Right," said Maggie. "At first I thought it was a ghost. But it was really the thief who escaped in the elevator and took over a bus."

"It *might* be a thief," corrected Mr. Pin.

"A ghost took over the bus?" asked Sally.

"No, the gargoyle smasher," said Maggie.

Mr. Pin was about to talk, but his beak was full of cinnamon roll.

"That's where I came in," said Gus.

"On the bus?" asked Sally.

"No," said Maggie. "Gus helped us *follow* the bus to the river. But the bridge went up and the thief got away."

"Mightfft mbe a thmief," said Mr. Pin. He tried to explain, but the cinnamon roll was making his beak stick together.

Suddenly the diner door swung open. It looked like the whole defensive line of the Chicago Bears had just walked in. But it was just

Sergeant O'Malley, a large policeman who liked to eat in the diner.

"Pin," he roared. "We're going to need your help." He strode over to a tray of cinnamon rolls and ate while he talked.

"Three gargoyles have fallen from buildings in this city, and the police are baffled."

"Baffled?" asked Mr. Pin, dabbing his beak with a napkin.

"Baffled," repeated O'Malley. "These gargoyles didn't fall by themselves. So far, no one has gotten hurt. But it could be dangerous."

"Hmmmm," said Mr. Pin. "Someone in Chicago must not like gargoyles."

"How's that?"

"Someone broke a gargoyle today in my uncle's warehouse," put in Maggie.

"Is that right?" said O'Malley.

"Looks like there's a gargoyle problem in this city," said Gus.

Mr. Pin nodded.

"One more thing," said O'Malley. "We found a chocolate box near the scene of one of the crimes. Thought you might be interested."

"Chocolate is always interesting," said Mr. Pin.

"The chocolate box was empty, and there were no fingerprints. Here, take a look."

"Too bad about the chocolate," said Mr. Pin as he took the box with one wing.

"We're on the case," said Maggie.

"Thanks," said O'Malley.

The sergeant left as suddenly as he had come in. Gus said he had to get back to his cab. That left Maggie to do her homework while Sally watched the diner. Mr. Pin went into his back room with the empty box of chocolate.

The penguin detective looked at the box closely. He held it up to his beak. Then, very carefully using tweezers, he removed what looked like a small speck of chocolate. He set the speck on a small glass slide and put it under a microscope. Cocking his head to one side, he adjusted the focus, then peered through the lens. Much to his surprise, he saw a secret message written in brown ink!

4

It was foggy again the next morning, and Mr. Pin had to think. He sat alone on a stool in Smiling Sally's with a plate of chocolate-chip pancakes.

Someone was going around the city smashing gargoyles. But why? And why was there only *part* of a message written inside an empty box of chocolate? It wasn't much to go on. But if he went back to the scene of the first crime, he might find a clue he had missed before. It was time to visit Uncle Otis.

Mr. Pin was about to look for Maggie when she came leaping down the back stairs, two at a time, red hair flying in all directions. Maggie had a way of not missing much.

"So where are we going today?" asked Maggie, watching Mr. Pin put on his red muffler and checked cap.

"Back to the warehouse," said Mr. Pin. "To look for more clues."

"Right," said Maggie. "It's a good thing I don't have school today." Maggie was about to ask Mr. Pin what the *first* clue was when Sally handed her a pancake sandwich (pancake on the outside, eggs on the inside) and a jacket. Then Maggie followed Mr. Pin out the door.

Otis seemed to be waiting for them at the warehouse. Although Maggie had her own key, her uncle was already at the door.

"He was here again!" said Maggie's uncle, wheezing as they rode upstairs in the creaking elevator.

"Who was here?" asked Maggie.

"The thief," said Otis.

"I don't think it was a thief," said Mr. Pin.

"Anyway," said Otis, "he was short and dark, and he smashed another gargoyle."

"I wonder why he doesn't like gargoyles?" said Maggie.

"Mind if I look around?" asked Mr. Pin as Otis pulled open the elevator door.

"Not at all," said Otis.

Mr. Pin opened his black bag and removed a pair of gloves.

Bzzzzzzz!!

"That's the door buzzer," said Otis.

While Otis rode the elevator back downstairs, Mr. Pin stooped down, picked something up off the floor, and put it into a plastic bag. He put the plastic bag into his black bag. Then he heard the rumble of the elevator again.

"Okay, Pin. What's going on?" It sounded like half of the Bears football team again, but it was just O'Malley, red-faced and sweating. O'Malley went on: "Another gargoyle was smashed late last night. Someone says that *you* were seen running from the scene of the crime. I don't understand how a crime-solving rock hopper could go so wrong, but now it's all beginning to make sense. Especially since we found another empty box of chocolate near the scene of the crime."

Mr. Pin thought about this. The shadowy figure that had escaped the warehouse and leaped onto the bus had been very short. Mr. Pin was about to suggest that he could not possibly have been in two places at once, but Maggie spoke first:

"Mr. Pin isn't the gargoyle smasher. *He's* trying to *find* the gargoyle smasher. In fact—"

"I can't believe it either," roared O'Malley, breaking in. "That's why I'm giving you twenty-four hours to prove I'm wrong. But in any case, you're off the case. And here's your box of chocolate."

Maggie and Otis stared in disbelief as O'Malley

tossed Mr. Pin another empty box, then stormed out of the warehouse. Strangely enough, Mr. Pin didn't look surprised. All he said was: "This could be exactly what I was looking for."

5

Late that night Maggie and Mr. Pin sat in his back room, looking at three empty chocolate boxes. Mr. Pin lined them up on his desk next to a microscope. A single light bulb dangling from the ceiling swung gently whenever the elevated train on Wabash went by.

"Just empty boxes of chocolate," said Maggie.

"Not quite," said Mr. Pin. "There's a clue in each one." Mr. Pin took out a pair of tweezers from his black bag. He held each box very carefully with gloves.

"I don't want to disturb any fingerprints," Mr. Pin said. "But I don't think I'll find any." Maggie watched as Mr. Pin removed what looked like a speck of chocolate from two of the boxes. Then he placed the two specks on microscope slides.

"I've already made a slide from the first box," explained Mr. Pin.

He held another slide up to his beak and said,

"It *looks* like chocolate, but it isn't. That's probably why no one thought it was important." Then he put the slide under the microscope lens.

"Now take a look at this," he said.

"Wow!" said Maggie. "There's a message. It says: IN GARGOYLE."

"Right," said Mr. Pin. "That was from the first box O'Malley gave me in the diner. Now read this one."

"CODEBOOK CLUE!" shouted Maggie.

"Now put the two messages together," said Mr. Pin.

"CODEBOOK CLUE IN GARGOYLE," said Maggie, reading the message. "Holy cow! Do you mean that . . . ?"

"Exactly," said Mr. Pin. "The gargoyle smasher is probably a spy. Who else would be looking for a codebook? Maybe even a government codebook."

"Which is hidden in a gargoyle."

"Not quite," explained Mr. Pin. "A *clue*, perhaps the most important clue, was hidden in a gargoyle. But no more."

"Why is that?" asked Maggie.

"The spy kept breaking gargoyles to find the last clue," said Mr. Pin. "If I'm not mistaken, that's the one O'Malley just found and gave to me at the warehouse. The spy found it, then put it in this chocolate box." Mr. Pin put a new slide under the lens and pointed with his wing for Maggie to look. "This is the clue," he said.

IN A LION SEEN BY MANY LIONS.
BE THERE AT MIDNIGHT.

Maggie looked at Mr. Pin, her eyes growing wider, and asked, "What in the world does it mean? There are lion gargoyles on buildings all over the city."

"I have an idea," said Mr. Pin. "There are two lion *statues* in front of the Art Institute. Across the street, on a building on Michigan Avenue, there are many more lions that look down on them."

"So which lion is the right one?" asked Maggie.

"I don't know," said Mr. Pin. "But I'm going to wait for the spy on the ground . . . not on the building across the street."

"Why is that?"

"Because penguins don't fly."

"This whole thing sounds fishy," said Maggie. "Why would a spy just accidentally drop his clues all over the place? Unless it's a trap to lure you someplace where the police will catch you."

"Exactly," said Mr. Pin. "And he thinks he'll get away with the codebook while the police hold me. So I'll just have to set my own trap. Tonight."

"It could be dangerous," said Maggie. "We have to tell the police."

"We can't," said Mr. Pin. "They think I'm involved."

"Then I'm going, too," said Maggie.

"Not this time," said Mr. Pin.

"So why are you telling me all of this if I can't go?" asked Maggie.

"In case," Mr. Pin said slowly, "I don't come back."

6

It was almost midnight. The streets were empty. A dark figure huddled under a black cape headed into the dense fog. He made his way across Wabash under the tracks toward Michigan Avenue.

Carrying a black bag, he inched behind a long, low wall of shrubs, then crouched down as he reached one of the statues in front of the Art

Institute. Slowly, he put his wing into the lion's mouth and took something out. He put it into his black bag. Then he took a roll of wire out of his bag and connected one end to the lion's tail and the other to the door of the Art Institute. He did the same thing with the other lion. Then he hid behind the first lion again.

Just in time.

Another dark figure slowly made his way up the stairs. When he reached the lion, he took a large mallet and chisel out of a brown bag and gripped one in each wing. He was about to hit the lion when Mr. Pin jumped out.

"Stop!" Mr. Pin shouted. "Don't hit that lion. Besides, it won't do you any good. It's bronze."

"What?!" said the spy with the chisel, still hidden in the fog. "So you finally caught up with me."

"You made it easy," said Mr. Pin. "Too easy."

"But my plan worked," said the spy. "The police think *you* are the gargoyle smasher."

"So that's why you left the clues," said Mr. Pin.

"Smart penguin," said the spy with a chuckle.

"Is that why you led me here, too?" asked Mr. Pin.

"No. That was an accident. I didn't mean to drop the last message. Even spies make mistakes."

"And coming here was a mistake, Mister—"

"You can call me Gargoyle," said the spy.

"Just one question, Gargoyle," said Mr. Pin. "Why the boxes of chocolate?"

"You and I are a lot alike," said the spy. He stepped out of the fog, and it all suddenly became clear to Mr. Pin how it could look as if he had been in two places at once.

The spy was a rock hopper penguin, too!

It was a lot to think about. But Mr. Pin didn't have time to think. Gargoyle lunged toward the statue, desperate for the codebook. The chisel glinted in the glow of the streetlight. Mr. Pin stepped aside. Gargoyle sprang forward and tripped on the wire. Alarms screeched. Museum guards rushed outside.

Gargoyle struggled to get up, then spun on his webbed feet. He sped down the stairs just as a bus pulled up, and he jumped on. Mr. Pin watched from the museum steps. And then, although he wasn't sure why, he raised the missing codebook to his brow and saluted the only other penguin who had ever walked the streets of Chicago. Gargoyle raised his wing, returning the salute as the bus, driven by a man in a trench coat, disappeared into the fog.

Meanwhile, O'Malley was first on the scene, along with Maggie, who had somehow forgotten about not calling the police. Most of the time, Maggie listened to Mr. Pin. But this wasn't one of those times.

Maggie jumped out while O'Malley hauled his large frame out of the squad car. Mr. Pin came down the stairs and handed O'Malley the book.

"This is what the gargoyle smasher was looking for," said Mr. Pin. "But it looks like he got away. Turns out he was a spy named Gargoyle. I found the book inside the lion's mouth. It was a good thing I got here first. It looked like he was going to hit the lion with a chisel. He didn't know I had already found the codebook."

"I'm just glad you're all right," said Maggie.

Mr. Pin explained to the museum guards and O'Malley what had happened, but O'Malley just kept shaking his head.

"I don't understand," he said. "You're here, but as I was driving up, I thought I saw a rock hopper penguin hop into a bus."

"You're right," said Mr. Pin. "And he may be back. *That* was the spy who came north from the Pole."

The Spitter Pitchers

1

Wrigley Field was hot. But it was hotter in the bleachers. The rock hopper penguin detective Mr. Pin and his friend Maggie were sitting under the scoreboard, watching the Cubs.

So far it was a close game with a lot at stake. The Cubs were in second place. The game they were playing against the Dodgers could put them in first.

"Frosty malt! Frosty malt!" called a vendor. It was unusual for someone to be selling ice cream in the bleachers. Mr. Pin held up his wing. A cold frosty malt came down the row, hand to hand, until it reached the penguin detective. Mr. Pin sent his money back the same way.

"Thanks," called Mr. Pin as he took the lid off the frosty malt. He was about to shovel the ice cream into his beak when he noticed some writing on the lid.

It was a message for him! Interesting, he thought. But it wouldn't be the first time he had found notes in strange places.

"Come to my office after the game," the note said. It was signed: "Walter Wavemin." Walter was the Cubs manager.

Mr. Pin ate the frosty malt but saved the lid. He dropped it into his black bag.

The Dodgers were up at bat. Runners were at the corners. And the game was tied 5 to 5 in the top of the seventh.

"Steeeeerike!" growled the umpire. The bleacher fans went wild. Someone threw peanut shells into the air. Maggie kept score on a pad of paper held on her lap.

"Ball one." The crowd was suddenly quiet.

After three more pitches, the count was full, and the batter fouled down the right field line.

The next pitch came in low, over the plate. The Dodgers' batter got behind the ball, and it rode the breezes toward the bleachers. Cubs fans gasped. An outfielder leaped but was unable to reach the homer. Several fans sprang eagerly for the ball. But it was a black wing that easily grabbed it out of the air and threw it back onto the field. A TV camera zoomed in.

"Nice wing on that penguin," said the outfielder as he tossed it to the shortstop.

Wavemin went to the mound. He called in

his ace relief pitcher Sam Spitter, hoping he could get the Cubs back in the game. Sam held the Dodgers in the eighth inning. But he let two runs score in the ninth. The Dodgers won 10 to 5.

"There's always the next game," said Maggie to Mr. Pin. "We're not out of the race yet."

"No. And we're not out of the park yet either," said Mr. Pin.

"What do you mean?"

"Walter Wavemin wants to see us," said Mr. Pin.

"Really!" said Maggie. "How do you know?"

"I was given a note on a frosty malt lid."

Many strange things had happened, thought Maggie, since Mr. Pin had come to live at her aunt Sally's diner. But never before had the manager of a major league baseball team written a note on a frosty malt lid asking to see Mr. Pin.

"Do you think the note is really from Walter Wavemin?" asked Maggie as the two detectives made their way through the crowd.

"There's only one way to find out," said Mr. Pin.

Maggie and Mr. Pin slipped through an unmarked door and went down a flight of stairs. They waited for some time until all of the players had gone home; then they went inside the locker room.

The room was shaped like a cylinder and smelled like bubble gum, wet towels, and sweaty athletic tape. Uniforms tumbled out of hampers, and a box of new baseballs had been left on a table along with an unfinished game of cards. Maggie and Mr. Pin made their way past the wooden lockers as the batboys came in to clean the players' spikes.

The two detectives walked down another hallway and up a flight of stairs to Wavemin's office. He was sitting behind a desk, a pile of bubble gum wrappers at his elbow.

"Detective Pin," said Mr. Pin. He tipped his checked cap and added: "Reasonable rates."

"You have quite a reputation as a crime solver and lover of chocolate," said Wavemin. "That's why I gave a note to a frosty malt vendor. I knew you were at the game and would be buying a lot of chocolate. He'd have no trouble spotting you."

"I like frosty malts," said Mr. Pin. "Especially chocolate. Now, what's the crime?"

"There isn't one yet," said Wavemin. "But something's not right with Sam Spitter. He's been getting strange phone calls here in the clubhouse. When anyone else answers and asks who it is, the caller hangs up. And just the other day I saw Sam putting on a fake mustache."

"Really!" said Maggie. She wrote what Wavemin had said on her pad of paper.

"Anything else?" asked Mr. Pin.

"He's in a slump," said Wavemin.

"Could happen," said Mr. Pin.

"But it can't happen now!" said Wavemin. He thumped his fist on his desk, and the wrappers flew up like a pile of leaves. "We're going to win the pennant this year."

"I understand. I'm on the case," said Mr. Pin as he hopped over an Ace bandage and left the manager's office with Maggie.

2

It was still crowded on Waveland Avenue as Maggie and Mr. Pin made their way from the ballpark through a cluster of people who were eating hot dogs and listening to a street-corner drummer.

"If there were any more people," said Maggie, "I think we'd stick together."

"Like penguins," commented Mr. Pin.

"Wait!" shouted Maggie. "Isn't that Sam Spitter?" At first the person she pointed to looked like an old man. He was bent over and had a gray beard. He wore overalls, dark glasses, and a mustache.

"I think that mustache is fake," said Mr. Pin.

Only Mr. Pin's and Maggie's sharp eyes for detail could detect the ace pitcher beneath the disguise.

"I wonder where he's going?" said Maggie.

"Quick," said Mr. Pin, spinning on his webbed feet. "I think he's headed north."

Maggie and Mr. Pin hurried after the disguised Sam Spitter, through the turnstile, up the stairs, and onto a train headed north.

It was a tight fit as the elevated train, or el, careened along its tracks. It was tricky, too, because Spitter was sitting next to the door. Maggie and Mr. Pin were at the back of the car behind a lot of tall people. At any moment, Sam could jump out, and if the detectives didn't move fast, he'd disappear before they could find out where he was going and why he was wearing a disguise.

It was several stops later that Mr. Pin suddenly said to Maggie, "This is our stop. Spitter's getting off."

Mr. Pin was able to wedge his way gently through the crowd with his beak while Maggie followed close behind. As they left the train, they saw Sam hurrying down the stairs toward a bus. Sam got on and sat in the back. Maggie and Mr. Pin made it just in time and sat toward the front.

Mr. Pin took a newspaper out of his black bag and held it up so they couldn't be seen. He didn't want the pitcher to know he was being followed.

But it wasn't long before Sam pulled the bus cord and got off. The two detectives rode to the next stop, left the bus, and doubled back. From a distance, they watched as Sam unlocked the gate of a Little League baseball park. Once inside, he relocked the gate.

Maggie looked up at a sign shaped like a giant baseball. It stood next to the park where hundreds of Little League teams would play that summer.

"Thillens!" said Maggie excitedly, reading the sign. "I played baseball here last summer. Pitched a no-hitter."

"I remember," said Mr. Pin.

"You helped me with my fastball," said Maggie.

Maggie and Mr. Pin weren't sure what a major league pitcher disguised as an old man was doing in a deserted Little League park. But they wanted to find out. Hiding close by in some bushes, Mr. Pin rested his beak on the chain-link fence. The two detectives watched to see what Sam would do.

Pretty soon a small truck pulled up. A man about the same height as Sam stepped out. He also unlocked the gate.

"If I didn't know better," said Maggie, "I could swear that man was also Sam Spitter."

"Maybe it is," said Mr. Pin.

Sam and the man who looked like Sam strode onto the field together. The man the detectives had followed on the el took off his dark glasses. Still wearing a beard, he put on a catcher's mitt, a mask, and a chest protector. He squatted behind the plate. The man from the truck went up to the mound. He started a windup.

Zinnnng! Smack. The ball sank into the catcher's glove.

"Nice!" said the catcher. "Fingers on the seams for a split-finger fastball."

The pitcher wound up again.

Zinnnng! Smack.

"Better," said the catcher.

"The man on the mound isn't Sam," whispered Mr. Pin to Maggie.

"How do you know?"

"Sam already knows how to throw a split-finger fastball."

"Now, don't work on the ball," said the catcher to the pitcher who wasn't Sam Spitter. "No nail marks, grease, or spit. There isn't time if you're a relief pitcher. Besides, it isn't right."

"Okay, Sam," said the pitcher. "The Spitter pitchers don't throw spitters."

"Right," said the catcher.

"So the catcher is Sam Spitter," whispered Maggie to Mr. Pin, clutching the chain-link fence. "But if Sam's the catcher and the pitcher looks just like him and his name is also Spitter, *who* is the pitcher?"

"His twin," said Mr. Pin calmly.

"Twin Spitter pitchers!" said Maggie. "I can't believe it!" It was a good thing a bus rolled by, or she might have been heard.

"But I don't think Sam wants anyone to know there are two of him. That's why he's wearing a disguise," explained Mr. Pin.

"Try the split-finger again," said Sam from behind his mask.

Zinnnng! Thud. This time the catcher couldn't catch the ball.

"Great!" yelled Sam. "Now you've got it. Remember to be at the park early next week for the night game."

"Thanks, Sam."

The two pitchers finished their practice as the sun set on Thillens Park. They packed their gear, locked the gate, and Sam's twin drove them away in the pickup truck.

As the two detectives walked back to the bus stop, Maggie said to Mr. Pin: "Sam's twin is a good pitcher."

"Very good," said Mr. Pin.

"He's as good as Sam," said Maggie.

"He's just as good," said Mr. Pin. "Especially if Sam's in a slump."

"The Cubs could win the pennant," said Maggie. "Maybe even the Series."

"With good pitching," said Mr. Pin to Maggie as the bus pulled up. "And I wonder . . . what will happen at that game next week?"

3

Back at the diner Mr. Pin spent most of the evening in his back room, putting together a small model of Wrigley Field. He had just finished the upper deck and was about to glue on the lights.

"Wrigley Field was the last of the old ballparks to put in lights," said Mr. Pin to Maggie.

"Why did they do it?" asked Maggie.

Mr. Pin held up the tiny cardboard lights with a tweezer and replied, "So people can find the frosty malt vendor."

"Seriously."

"So the players can find the dugout at night," Mr. Pin went on. "So the manager can see who's pitching."

Maggie wasn't sure she was going to get a real answer about the lights that night from Mr. Pin. So she left Mr. Pin muttering something about "all the great old ballparks, and old Wrigley didn't want the lights after all." Maggie went upstairs to feed her gerbils.

Mr. Pin looked at his model of Wrigley Field.

He held the lights in his tweezers and thought out loud: "If the lights are on, the manager can see who's pitching. But if the lights are off, no one knows who's on the mound. Very interesting. I wonder . . ."

It was growing late, and the Sox were playing on the coast. The game was on the radio. "Now here's the pitch," said the announcer. Mr. Pin wadded up a piece of paper. Then the rock hopper penguin went into a spectacular windup, pivoted on his webbed feet, and slammed a sinker into a wastebasket.

"There are no minor leagues at the South Pole," said Mr. Pin.

4

The sky was dark. But the lights were on at Wrigley Field.

It was an important game for the Cubs. It could also be an important game for Sam Spitter. Sam had told his brother to come early to this night game. Something just didn't feel right to Mr. Pin. So he called Walter and told him he would be at this game. When the manager gave

47

Mr. Pin two free tickets behind the Cubs dugout, the penguin detective didn't complain.

"Bill 'the Babe' Bruseball is starting pitcher," said Maggie to Mr. Pin. She was listening to a play-by-play on a radio headset.

"Sam Spitter is in the bull pen, ready for relief if the Cubs need him," said Mr. Pin, enjoying his first frosty malt.

"Right," said Maggie. "I wonder how many innings Bruseball will pitch before they bring in Sam."

"I hope he doesn't pitch," said Mr. Pin.

"Do you really think something is going to happen?"

"Absolutely."

Maggie put her elbows on her knees and watched as the game began. The Cubs were only one-half game out of first. If they won this game, they would be tied for first and might win the division. But Mr. Pin had said that something strange might happen to one of the Cubs pitchers. It was enough to make anyone nervous.

Mr. Pin bought his second frosty malt.

Berta Largamente was singing the "The Star-Spangled Banner" while Maggie fumbled with her Cubs program. Mr. Pin had solved a case for Berta when a conductor disappeared in a cloud of blue smoke. But that was another story.

The game was slow and tense. The Mets and the Cubs traded runs for six innings, and the score was tied 4 to 4. Mr. Pin had decided to limit himself to one frosty malt each inning. But the innings were long, and Mr. Pin was getting hungry fast. There didn't seem to be a vendor in sight, so the rock hopper penguin told Maggie he would be back, and he set out to find one.

Mr. Pin headed up the concrete aisle, peanut shells crunching beneath his feet. He looked to each side and, just a few rows ahead, spotted a vendor carrying a cool case of frosty malts. Mr. Pin paid the vendor and was about to return to his seat when a foul ball flew over the dugout in his direction. With a quick hop, Mr. Pin snagged the ball out of the air. The crowd roared.

"Great fielding from that penguin," said the announcer.

"Nice catch," said the vendor.

And that was when Mr. Pin suddenly realized who the vendor really was.

"Sam Spitter!" said Mr. Pin, twirling the ball on the tip of his wing.

"Shhhh," said Sam. "Don't let anyone know who I am."

"I almost *didn't* know who you were," said Mr. Pin. Sam was wearing another disguise: a long gray wig that hung over his eyes and large black-framed glasses that covered most of the rest of his face. A fake nose was cleverly attached to his glasses.

"Why are you wearing a costume?" asked Mr. Pin.

"I'm selling frosty malts," said Sam.

"A good job, but you might need to pitch soon."

"I'm not pitching this game," said Sam.

Suddenly everyone stood up and started yelling like crazy.

"Out of the park," said Mr. Pin. "The Cubs are ahead now by one run."

"They won't need a relief pitcher yet," said Sam over the roar of fans.

"What happens if they do?" asked Mr. Pin.

Sam wouldn't answer.

But Mr. Pin already knew. "Your brother's going to pitch, isn't he?" It wasn't really a question. "He's warming up in the bull pen while you're out here selling frosty malts. I also know why. But even though your brother's a great pitcher, you're the one who has to pitch."

"I can't. This is the worst slump I've ever been in. I'd lose it for the Cubs. And how do you know my brother can pitch?" asked Sam.

"Thillens."

"You were there?" asked Sam.

"With my partner," said Mr. Pin. "Anyway, I think Wavemin would give your brother a chance if I talked to him."

"You would do that? He never had the chance to try out that I did. He had chicken pox and a pulled hamstring the day the scout came."

"No problem," said Mr. Pin. "I do know that if your brother—"

"Slim."

"Right," Mr. Pin went on. "If your brother Slim wins the game, somebody'd find out and the Cubs would forfeit. You'd be doing the wrong thing for the right reasons. Slim will get his chance. I'll see that he does."

With the Cubs' third out, the organ began to play and the Mets left the field. Bill ("the Babe") Bruseball went to the mound. Mr. Pin and Sam watched as the Babe threw a fastball and narrowly missed the batter. The next pitch hit the batter, sending him to first.

Then the Babe hit the next batter, too, putting the leading run on first and the tying run on second.

"He won't be up much longer if he keeps hitting batters," said Sam. "Seems always to happen to the Babe when he gets tired."

Bruseball hit the third batter. The bases were loaded. Wavemin went to the mound.

Bruseball stared into the lights and rubbed his forehead with his cap. A breeze came off the lake. The park looked like a stage with Bruseball standing in the middle surrounded by spotlights. For now, it seemed that Wavemin was going to leave him in.

"Quick," said Mr. Pin. "We don't have much time. Sam, I know how good you are if you just give yourself a chance. You can't give up because you're in a slump. Keep your fingers on the seams and just get out there and play because you love the Cubs and you love baseball."

It was then that Mr. Pin looked down the aisle and saw Maggie buying a bag of peanuts. Mr. Pin caught her eye and pointed with his wing to the vendor. Maggie hurried over.

"Sam!" she said. "What are you doing here?"

"I am afraid there isn't time to explain," Mr. Pin said to Maggie. "I need your help." He drew what looked like a very small map of the ballpark on a frosty malt lid. He pointed to a spot marked with an X.

"This is where you're going," said Mr. Pin. "When you get inside, watch the monitor. When Wavemin goes to the mound a second time, count to sixty. Then turn these dials. They look like the round knobs on a stove. I've drawn a picture so you know what to expect. Count to sixty again and turn them back."

"Am I turning off all the lights?" asked Maggie.

"Precisely," said Mr. Pin.

"But why . . . ?"

"I'm afraid I can't tell you now," said Mr. Pin.

"All right," said Maggie as she hurried down the concrete ramp, studying the map as she went.

"Sam, come this way," said Mr. Pin. "And bring your frosty malts."

Sam followed Mr. Pin to the box seats near the dugout. Wavemin had given Bruseball one more chance. But it was a mistake. The Babe went into his windup and threw a perfect strike. Unfortunately, the Mets hitter met it with incredible force. The crowd groaned as they

watched the ball sail over the bleachers and out of the park. The score was 8 to 5. It looked like real trouble for the Cubs.

Wavemin went to the mound. Bruseball had thrown his last pitch.

"When I give the signal," said Mr. Pin, "hop over the wall and head for the mound."

Bruseball was on his way back to the dugout. Wavemin signaled for who he thought was Sam to come in. Then all of a sudden the lights at Wrigley Field went out.

"Now!" shouted Mr. Pin.

It couldn't have been easy for a rock hopper penguin to convince Slim to trade clothes with his brother and become a frosty malt vendor all in sixty seconds. But somehow Mr. Pin was able to do it.

When the lights went back on, Sam was on the mound tying his shoes, Slim was walking up the aisle yelling, "Frosty malts," and Mr. Pin was walking back across the infield toward his seat. The fans weren't sure who the short new manager eating a frosty malt was, but it didn't seem to matter.

Sam held the Mets at 8 to 5. In the bottom of the eighth the Cubs loaded the bases with Sam at bat. It didn't happen very often and might not happen again for a long time . . . but Sam hit a grand slam. Walter Wavemin went crazy. He jumped up and down and waved his arms in circles, hurrying the runners home. Sam's homer went over the bleachers onto Waveland Avenue and landed somewhere near a peanut vendor.

As for Slim, Mr. Pin convinced the manager to give Sam's twin brother a chance to try out for the Cubs. Wavemin said the Cubs didn't need any more relief pitchers since Sam was well out of his slump, but he said he'd see what he could do.

A few days later Walter Wavemin called Mr. Pin and offered him a job. "I saw you catch that foul. I could use a fielder like you," he said. "You have a great left wing."

"That's all right," Mr. Pin told him. "There's plenty of work coming by the diner to keep me busy. But what happened with Sam's brother? Has anyone signed him yet?"

"Sure," said Wavemin.

"Who?" asked Mr. Pin.

"The Minnesota Twins," Wavemin said. "Now, are you sure you won't play for the Cubs?"

"No, thanks," said Mr. Pin. "But someday . . ."

"What's that?" Walter asked.

"If a young lady with red hair named Maggie shows up and wants to try out, give her a chance. She has a mean fastball. Not only that, but she's one smart kid in a city that loves baseball, and she knows how to keep her fingers on the seams."